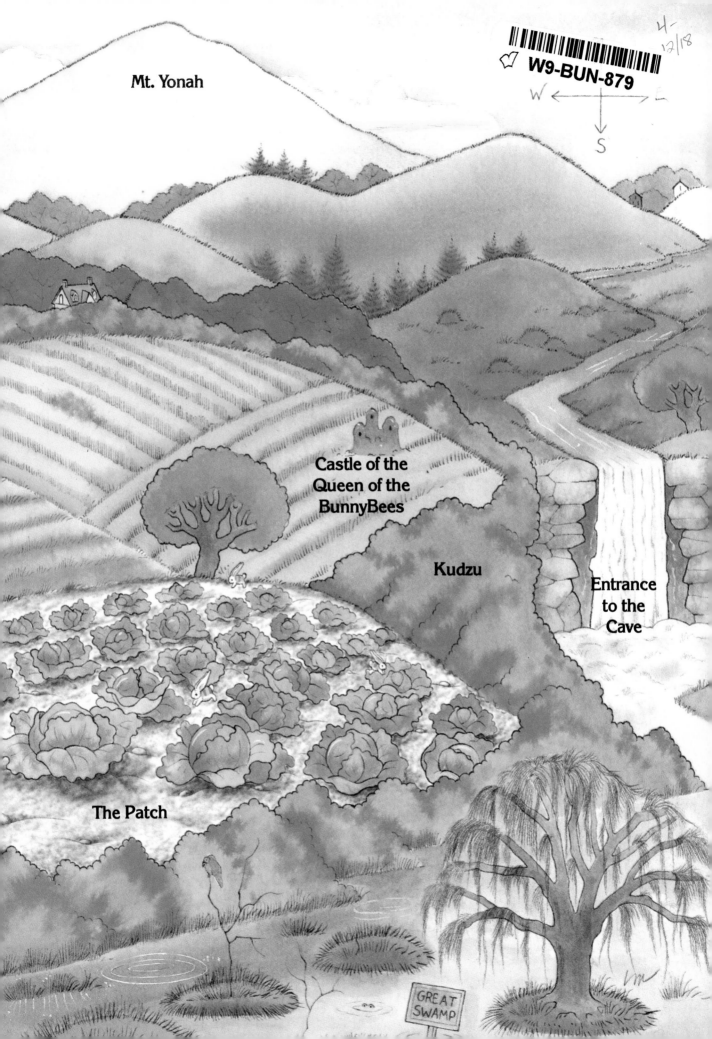

Copyright © 1984 Original Appalachian Artworks, Inc. Published in the United States by Parker Brothers, Division of CPG Products Corp. Cabbage Patch Kids™ and the character names contained in this book are trademarks of and licensed from Original Appalachian Artworks, Inc. Cleveland, GA. U.S.A. All rights reserved.

Library of Congress Cataloging in Publication Data: Daly, Kathleen N. Making friends. (Cabbage Patch kids). SUMMARY: With the help of Rachel Marie, Otis Lee and Rebecca Ruby come to appreciate each other's differences and become friends.
[1. Bullies—Fiction.]   I. Cocca-Leffler, Maryann, ill.   II. Title.   III. Series.
PZ7.D1696Mak   1984   [E]   83-25118   ISBN 0-910313-27-X
Manufactured in the United States of America   1 2 3 4 5 6 7 8 9 0

Making Friends

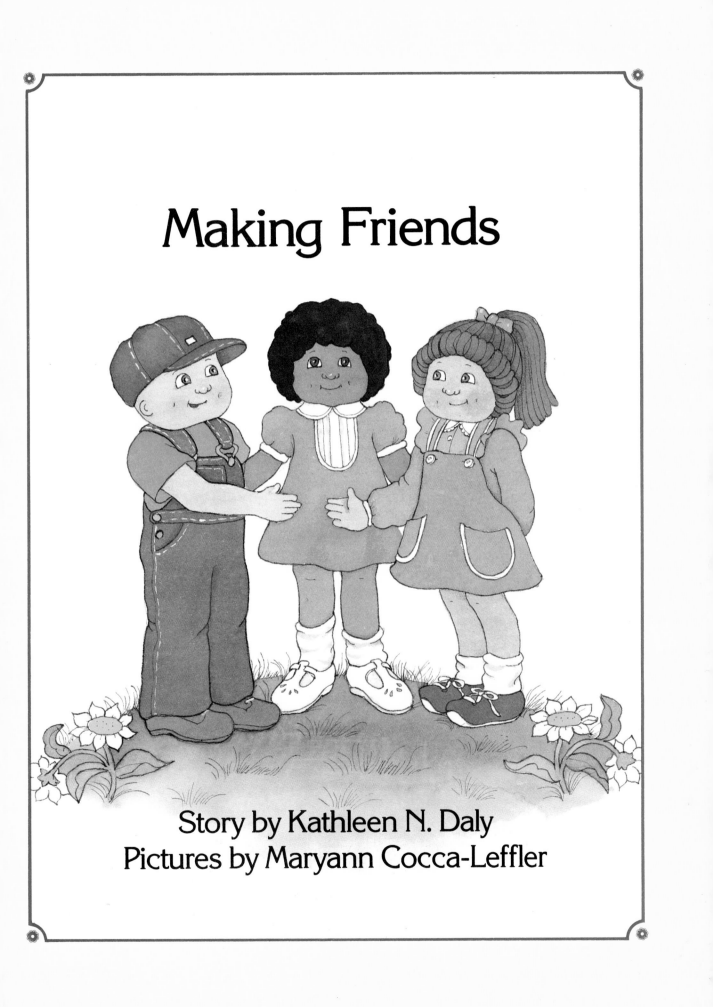

Story by Kathleen N. Daly
Pictures by Maryann Cocca-Leffler

Each of the Cabbage Patch Kids was quite different from all the others. No two were more different from each other, however, than Otis Lee and Rebecca Ruby. For example, Otis Lee didn't have any hair on his head, and Rebecca Ruby had so much hair that she wore bangs and a ponytail.

Otis Lee and Rebecca Ruby had very different critters that they loved. Otis Lee had a bulldog named Cap'n. Cap'n could be ferocious and fast. Rececca Ruby had a turtle named *Miss Myrtle. Miss Myrtle* was always very gentle and slow.

Otis Lee rode a dirt bike. He loved to patrol the Cabbage Patch and keep on the lookout for the black-hearted jackrabbit, Cabbage Jack and sneaky Beau Weasel, who both worked for the wicked Lavendar McDade.

Rebecca Ruby was timid. She liked to pick flowers for the Castle of the Queen of the BunnyBees. Most of all, she liked to skip rope, which she did all the time. Rebecca Ruby thought that if everybody would be kind, everybody would get along. She even thought the 'Kids and the BunnyBees should be kind to Lavendar McDade and her crew of cutthroats and invite them to visit.

"Kind to Lavendar?" snorted Otis Lee, when Rebecca Ruby told him what she thought. "Are you crazy? Invite those rascals to visit! They would probably poison us!"

"Well, maybe we could send Lavendar a note and ask her to promise to be friends and try to get along with us," suggested Rebecca Ruby timidly.

Otis Lee was so astonished that he blurted out,
"Rebbeca Ruby, are you just plain dumb, or do you practice
being stupid while you skip rope?"

Rebecca Ruby hated to be yelled at. She was so hurt by
Otis Lee's words that she answered back, "At least I'm
not a bully like you! I don't go around making a horrible racket
with a horrible old dirt bike that churns up dust everywhere!"

Otis Lee gave Rebecca Ruby a look of disgust, got on his dirt bike, and rode off with a roar. Rebecca Ruby felt terrible. That awful Otis Lee had hurt her feelings and made her lose her temper.

Rebecca Ruby tried to pick flowers, but she could only think about what Otis Lee had called her — dumb. She tried to skip rope, but she was too upset. She tried to play with Miss Myrtle, but Miss Myrtle pulled her head and legs into her shell. Rebecca Ruby felt that no one loved her at all, and she sat down under a tree and cried.

Georgia Ann walked over and asked, "What's wrong, Rebecca Ruby?"

"Everything," Rebecca Ruby wept.

Georgia Ann hated to see Rebecca Ruby cry, so she went to Rachel Marie and told her all about it.

Rachel Marie who was called Ramie, was one of the older Cabbage Patch Kids. She was very wise about many things and loved to tell the others about life in the old days, when no one had ever heard of the horrible and mean Lavendar McDade. Those were the days when there was peace and love everywhere, and babies born in the Cabbage Patch grew up happy and safe.

"Let me look into this," said Ramie. "Otis Lee and Rebecca Ruby never seem to get along."

Ramie found Rebecca Ruby under the tree, still crying. She sat down beside her. "Rebecca Ruby, why are you crying?" she asked.

"Otis Lee doesn't like me," sobbed Rebecca Ruby. "He thinks I'm stupid."

"Why would Otis Lee think that?" asked Ramie gently.

Rebecca Ruby put her head on Ramie's shoulder and told her what had happened.

When Rebecca Ruby had told her everything, Ramie replied, "Perhaps Otis Lee is so worried about the danger we face from Lavendar that he doesn't realize you would like to find a way for there to be peace."

"Otis Lee just likes to make noise and be angry." Rebecca Ruby insisted. "He rides that dirt bike around the Cabbage Patch all the time."

"That's because he wants to protect us," said Ramie. "If you want peace, I think a good way to begin is to have peace between you and Otis Lee."

"How?" asked Rebecca Ruby.

"I'm not sure," said Ramie. "Maybe you could do something that Otis Lee would admire. You could show him that you don't dislike him or his dirt bike."

"I don't like that dirt bike," said Rebecca Ruby. "It's noisy and scares me."

"Hmmm," said Ramie. "What if you weren't scared of the dirt bike? What if you could ride it as well as Otis Lee? What would Otis Lee think of you then?"

"I guess he'd think I wasn't so dumb," said Rebecca Ruby.

Ramie smiled and stood up. "Rebecca Ruby," she said, "It's time you and Otis Lee were friends. I'll see you later." And off she went, smiling to herself.

Ramie walked to the far side of the Cabbage Patch. Sure enough, along came Otis Lee, riding as fast as a whirlwind, with the dust flying up behind him. He screeched the dirt bike to a stop when he saw Ramie waving to him.

"Don't go outside the 'Patch, Ramie," warned Otis Lee. "Beau Weasel and Cabbage Jack sometimes sneak around close as they dare, hoping to catch some of us 'Kids."

"The way you patrol the Cabbage Patch," laughed Ramie, "I should think those scoundrels would be sure to stay away."

Otis Lee grinned. Ramie had a way of making folks feel good about themselves.

"I've been talking to Rebecca Ruby," said Ramie.

"Have you, now?" mumbled Otis Lee.

"Yes," said Ramie. "The poor child was crying hard enough to make a puddle of tears."

"And I guess you know why," said Otis Lee.

"I sure do," said Ramie.

"I feel bad about calling her stupid," said Otis Lee. "But she made me mad. Of all the dumb things to say, she said we should invite Lavendar McDade to visit!"

Ramie laughed. "Well, that wasn't a very good idea, I agree. But Rebecca Ruby wants everybody to be peaceful. She doesn't realize how wicked Lavendar can really be. She doesn't understand how hard you work to protect us. And the dirt bike scares her with its noise and dust."

"I can't do a thing about how Rebecca Ruby feels,"
muttered Otis Lee.

"You could *try*," said Ramie.

"How?" asked Otis Lee.

"Try doing something that she would admire. You could
show her that you don't dislike her or what she does."

"All she does is skip rope," muttered Otis Lee.

"I suppose you think it's easy to skip rope," said Ramie.

"Nothing's easier," said Otis Lee.

"That's what you think," said Ramie. "But no one can jump rope anywhere near as well as Rebecca Ruby."

Otis Lee guffawed a big guffaw. "I figure *I* can," he boasted.

"But no one can skip harder or higher or longer than she," insisted Ramie.

"Listen, I could skip rope any old way for as long as you'd want," said Otis Lee. "Skipping rope is nothing compared to riding a dirt bike."

"Prove it," said Ramie. "Rebecca Ruby should admire anybody who could skip rope as well as she can."

"Give me a day to practice and I will," said Otis Lee.

"Okay," said Ramie. "Can I have the loan of your dirt bike while you are practicing skipping rope?"

"Sure," said Otis Lee. "I trust you to be careful with it."

The next day, Otis Lee went way off by himself with a rope and began to practice skipping.

Ramie took the dirt bike and got Rebecca Ruby to go along with her to a place where they were alone. She began to teach Rebecca Ruby to ride.

That day, Rebecca Ruby and Otis Lee each worked very hard to learn something new.

That night, everyone noticed how tired Otis Lee was. They saw how tired Rebecca Ruby was. Even Ramie looked all done in.

Otis Lee stared at Rebecca Ruby. He thought, "Skipping rope *isn't* easy. If she can skip rope better than I can, she must be terrific."

Rebecca Ruby glanced at Otis Lee when he wasn't looking. She knew her idea about inviting Lavendar to visit was pretty silly. She thought to herself, "I fell off the bike a lot today. Anybody who rides that dirt bike as well as Otis Lee must be really strong and brave."

Early the next morning, Rebecca Ruby went out to skip rope under her favorite tree. She waved to Ramie, who was playing nearby. Just then, Otis Lee rode up on his dirt bike. Otis Lee and Rebecca Ruby stared at each other. Otis Lee suddenly said to Rebecca Ruby, "I'm sorry I called you stupid the other day."

"That's okay," said Rebecca Ruby. "I'm sorry about what I said. Want to skip rope?"

"Why not?" said Otis Lee.

They began to skip rope. When Otis Lee jumped hard, Rebecca Ruby jumped harder. When Otis Lee jumped high, Rebecca Ruby jumped higher. When Otis Lee jumped long, Rebecca Ruby jumped longer.

Finally, Otis Lee sat down, all out of breath. "You're the best rope skipper in the whole world, Rebecca Ruby," he said.

"Well, I do it all the time," she admitted. "But you're the only person who can skip near as well as me."

"Riding a dirt bike is tough," said Otis Lee. "I can't skip rope as well as you, but I can ride a dirt bike better than anybody."

"I can ride a dirt bike, too," said Rebecca Ruby.
"I don't believe it," he said.
"I'll show you," said Rebecca Ruby.

Before Otis Lee could say another word, she jumped on his dirt bike and took off *fast*! She roared across the grass and sent the 'Kids sprawling to get out of her way. She went faster and faster and made more and more noise. On her way back to the tree, it looked as if she would run right into it!

But at the last moment she missed the tree and went around it in ten circles until she finally managed to hit the brakes. She stopped so fast that she somersaulted through the air straight into Otis Lee and knocked him down.

"Gosh!" exclaimed Otis Lee. "You rode that dirt bike like a streak of lightning!"

"I can ride, but not as good as you," said Rebecca Ruby. She laughed, "And stoppping isn't so easy."

Ramie and the others ran over to see if they were all right.

"Did you all see Rebecca Ruby ride my dirt bike?" said Otis Lee. "She was really going like greased lightning!"

"You should see Otis Lee skip rope," said Rebecca Ruby. "He can outjump a grasshopper."

Ramie said, "Otis Lee and Rebecca Ruby are certainly a pair! They're our best two rope skippers and our best two dirt bikers, if you ask me."

Everybody clapped and cheered. Ramie said it was such a wonderful day that they could all play hide and seek together, or let Otis Lee give them rides on his dirt bike, or let Rebecca Ruby teach them how to skip rope. And that is exactly what they did all morning.

"You helped Otis Lee and Rebecca Ruby become friends," Georgia Ann said to Ramie. "How did you do it?"

"Oh, they did it themselves," said Ramie. "Sometimes friendship is just like a garden. A little care and love make it grow. I just helped them see how much care they could give each other."

Then she smiled and ran to join the others.

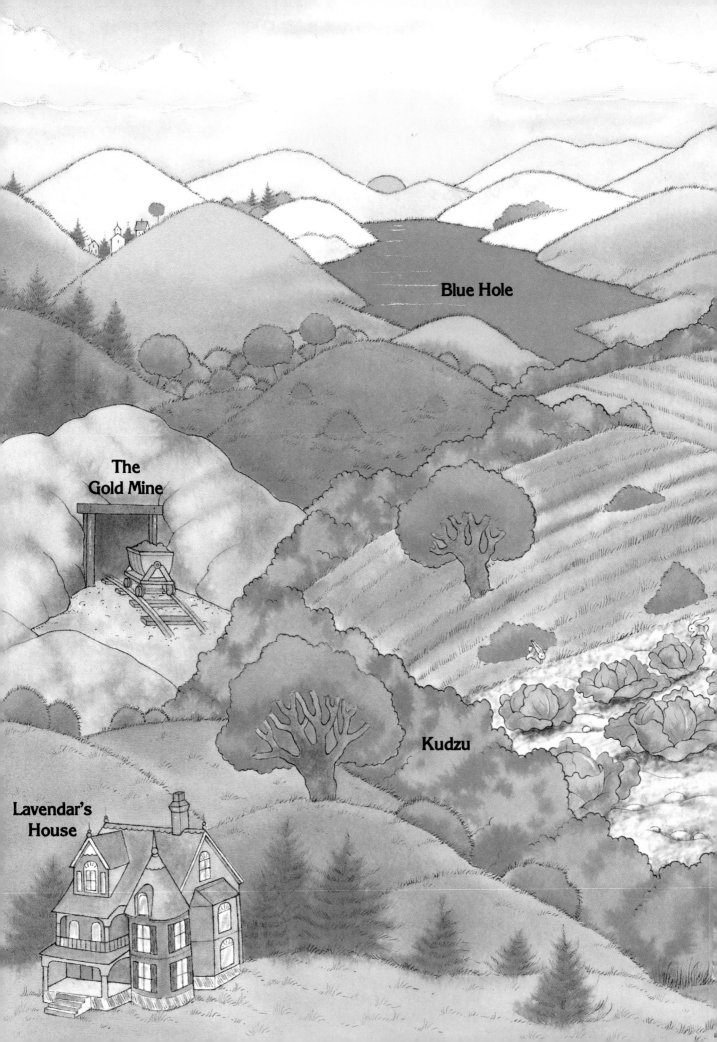